JJ,
Christmas 2020
Love
Mummy

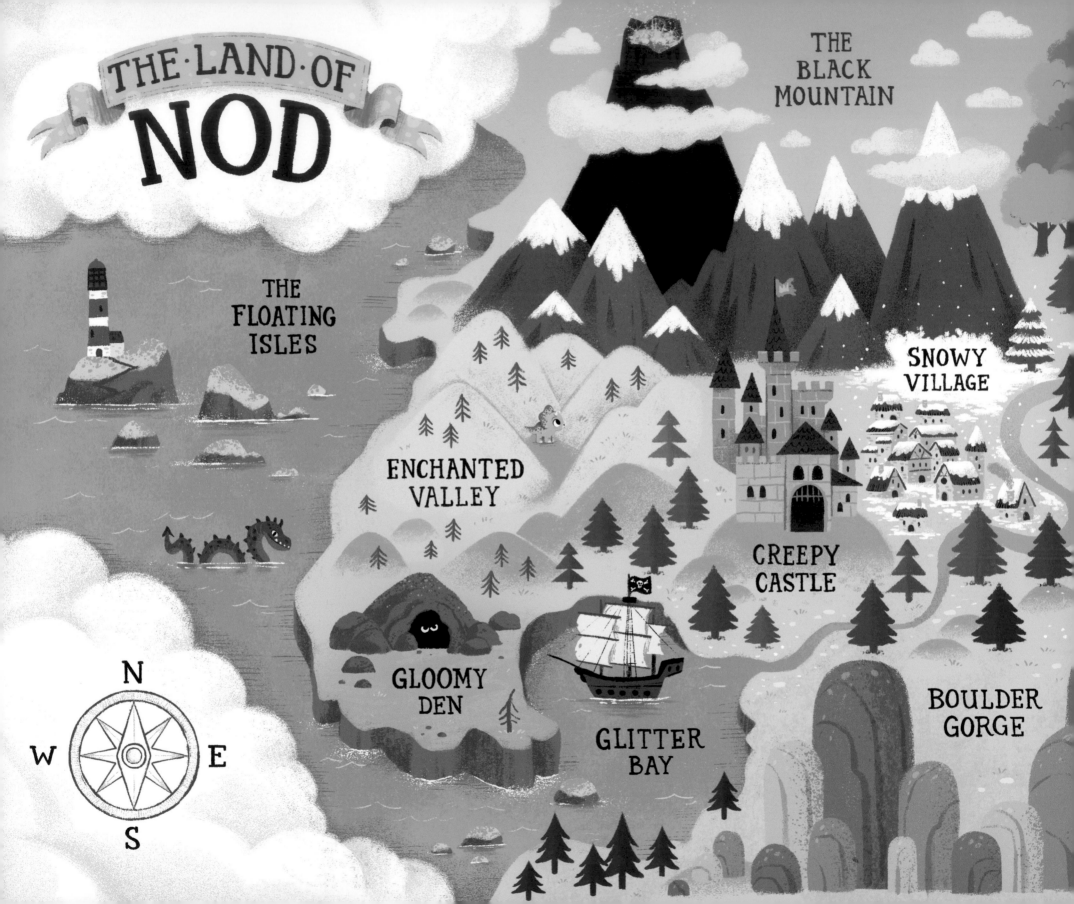

THE
ANCIENT FOREST

OUTER
SPACE

EMERALD
GLEN

DEADLY
CREEK

GIANTS' TOWN

THE
STINKY
SWAMPS

GOLDEN
COVE

RICKETY
BRIDGE

For Mat.
R.F.

For Sebastian.
C.C.

LADYBIRD BOOKS

UK | USA | Canada | Ireland | Australia | India | New Zealand | South Africa
Ladybird Books is part of the Penguin Random House group of companies
whose addresses can be found at global.penguinrandomhouse.com.
www.penguin.co.uk   www.puffin.co.uk   www.ladybird.co.uk

Penguin
Random House
UK

First published 2020
003
Written by Rhiannon Fielding. Text copyright © Ladybird Books Ltd, 2020
Illustrations copyright © Chris Chatterton, 2020
Moral rights asserted
Printed in Great Britain
A CIP catalogue record for this book is available from the British Library
ISBN: 978–0–241–38673–6
All correspondence to:
Penguin Random House Children's
One Embassy Gardens, 8 Viaduct Gardens,
London SW11 7BW

FSC
www.fsc.org
MIX
Paper from
responsible sources
FSC® C018179

TEN MINUTES TO BED

Little Dinosaur

Rhiannon Fielding • Chris Chatterton

In a **faraway land**, across mountains and seas,
where **strange creatures** live among tall jungle trees,
there can often be heard a **great echoing roar:**

With three pointed horns and four great big feet,
Rumble was crashing around in the heat.
"Nine minutes to bed! Don't go far!"
warned his mum,

but this little dinosaur
loved to have fun.

Deep in the jungle, a **hullabaloo!**

Frogs hopped about as birds fluttered and flew.

"Eight minutes to bed!"
came the call, loud and strong,
as Rumble the dinosaur
thundered
along.

Splashing about
in a warm pool of mud,

and chasing his tail
till he fell with a

THUD!

He knew there were just **seven minutes** to bed,
but Rumble preferred an **adventure**, instead.

Passing through mountains, he heard a **strange sound**; the world seemed to **tremble** from deep underground. He looked to the sky, with **six minutes to go . . .**

and saw a volcano

beginning to glow.

From the sky came a roar! Rumble stumbled and ducked –

BOOM!

The volcano began to erupt!

Hot lava bubbled,
    the sky filled with ash –
    rocks crumbled and fell to the ground
    with a crash.

From out of the valley poured dinosaurs small,
dinosaurs **heavy** and dinosaurs **tall**.
The ground below shook
as they all hurtled past:

"Five minutes," they said,
"so you'd better run fast!"

As he ran, with his heart
beating fast in his chest,

Rumble **finally** saw
a safe place he could rest.

"Four minutes to bed . . . but where am I, I wonder?"
From high in the sky
came a loud roll of thunder.

Below a great mountain,

where birds swoop and soar,

lay Rumble, the littlest dinosaur.

"Three minutes to bed,"
said a voice from the gloom,
and a **shadow** appeared
by the light of the moon.

On four great big feet,
she bent down to her son –
Rumble opened his eyes . . .
and looked up at his mum.

"Two minutes,"
she said.
"You are never alone."

Then at last, side by side,
   they both **plodded back home**.

The evening was bathed in a soft silver light
as his mum tucked him up
and she kissed him goodnight.
"One minute to bed –
that means no more exploring!"

But
Rumble . . .

. . . was already fast asleep, snoring.

THE·LAND·OF
NOD

THE
BLACK
MOUNTAIN

THE
FLOATING
ISLES

SNOWY
VILLAGE

ENCHANTED
VALLEY

CREEPY
CASTLE

GLOOMY
DEN

GLITTER
BAY

BOULDER
GORGE

THE
ANCIENT FOREST

OUTER
SPACE

EMERALD
GLEN

DEADLY
CREEK

GIANTS' TOWN

THE
STINKY
SWAMPS

GOLDEN
COVE

RICKETY
BRIDGE

Look out for more
bedtime adventures
in

Have you met Twinkle the unicorn . . .

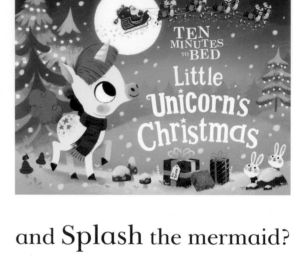

Belch the monster . . .

and Splash the mermaid?

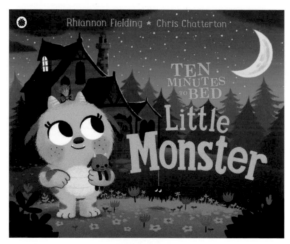